SEE YOU AT THE MATCH

Neil wants to be a footballer when he grows up but that means he's got to keep practising all the time, and one Saturday his football practice nearly makes him miss the match as he runs round the town doing errands for everyone! All because he kicked his football into the canal!

All these stories are about real football fans. One boy scores the winning goal, and one young girl has all the excitement of going to her first real game. But there's also disappointment – young Sam is bitterly upset because he can't see his all-time football hero play, and Joey discovers that your favourite team can't always win. Here are tales about professionals and amateurs – and even about one team who win with the help of a herd of cows!

Margaret Joy was born on Tyneside. After living for some years on Teesside, where she taught in a sixth-form college and later became a full-time teacher of five-year-olds, she moved to north Wales, where her husband is headmaster of a school for deaf children. They have four children. Margaret Joy has contributed many stories to BBC TV's *Play School* and BBC radio's *Listen with Mother*.

Other books by Margaret Joy

TALES FROM ALLOTMENT LANE SCHOOL
ALLOTMENT LANE SCHOOL AGAIN
HAIRY AND SLUG

SEE YOU
AT THE MATCH

Margaret Joy

Illustrated by Thelma Lambert

Puffin Books
in association with
Faber and Faber

Puffin Books, Penguin Books Ltd, Harmondsworth, Middlesex, England
Viking Penguin Inc., 40 West 23rd Street, New York, New York 10010, U.S.A.
Penguin Books Australia Ltd, Ringwood, Victoria, Australia
Penguin Books Canada Ltd, 2801 John Street, Markham, Ontario, Canada L3R 1B4
Penguin Books (N.Z.) Ltd, 182–190 Wairau Road, Auckland 10, New Zealand

First published by Faber and Faber 1985
Published in Puffin Books 1987

Printed and bound in Great Britain by
Cox & Wyman Ltd, Reading

for
David,
Aidan and Damian

Contents

'See You at the Match'

Neil was in the back yard, kicking his football against the brick wall. Kick-thud, back to him; kick-thud, back to him... He loved practising kicking like this. He wanted to be a footballer when he grew up. His Dad thought it was a good idea, too.

'But you'll have to keep practising,' he said. 'The more football you play, the better you'll get. And you can come along to watch a match with me on a Saturday afternoon sometimes, if you like. Then you can watch how the professionals play.'

'Cor, thanks, Dad. When? When will you take me?'

'Soon, soon. I'll tell you when a good match is coming up.'

Now, today was the day. Dad was going to take him to the match in an hour's time. So that was why Neil was in the back yard —

he was just waiting for his Dad to say it was time to set off. Neil started kicking again: kick-thud, back to him; kick-thud, back to him; kick-thud –

'Whoops! Hey, oh help!'

He had kicked the ball rather harder than before and it had spun sideways over the back-yard wall. Neil raced to climb on top of the dustbin in the corner of the yard and peered over the wall. He was just in time to see the ball rolling across the towpath and – splashhh! – into the canal.

'Oh no,' he groaned.

The ball was floating in the water. How on earth could he get it back? He wasn't allowed to go on the towpath by himself, it was too dangerous. But he wanted his football – what could he do?

He looked along the canal to one side of him. There was no one in sight, only a dog wandering along. He looked the other way. A long flat barge was slowly gliding along the canal towards him. A man was leaning on the side, smoking a pipe. He saw Neil peering over the top of the wall, then he saw the football in front of the barge, floating in

the water. He went to the back of the barge and it slowly came to a stop. The man came up on to the side again.

'Your football, is it?' he called to Neil.

'Yes, yes. Please can you get it for me?' said Neil. 'I'm not allowed on the towpath, it's dangerous, but I want my football back before I go to a match with my Dad.'

'Well, I'll fish it out for you all right,' said the man, 'but you've reminded me that it's Saturday afternoon — you lose track of what day it is when you're afloat — and I don't know what matches are being played today.

3

Will you pop to a paper shop and get me a paper with the sports news?'

Neil nodded. There was a newsagent's shop just at the end of his street, and he was allowed to go there by himself.

'Watch out!' said the man. He threw a fifty pence piece over the towpath, over the wall, and into Neil's back yard. It landed on the concrete with a clatter.

'Shan't be long,' called Neil. He scrambled down off the dustbin and picked up the fifty pence piece. He ran through the house to the front door.

'Shan't be long,' he called to his Dad. 'I'm just going to the paper shop.'

When he got there he said:

'Please can I have a paper with all this afternoon's sport in?'

'Course you can, sonny,' said the man. Then he looked at Neil.

'That reminds me,' he said. 'I told the wife I'd buy a jar of coffee, so she could make me a flask to take to the match. I'm shutting up shop in a few minutes' time, so I can rush home and get ready for the match. Could you just pop next door to the grocer's for me

and buy me a jar of coffee? Here's the money
— I'll have your paper and change ready for
you when you get back.'

Neil rushed next door to the grocer's and
said:

'Please can I have a jar of coffee for
the man in the paper shop, so his wife can
make him a flask of coffee to take to the
match?'

'Course you can, laddie,' said the grocer.
Then he looked at Neil. 'But that reminds me
— I've not got much change in the till, I'm
afraid, and I'll be needing some myself to
buy a programme on the way to the match.
I'll be shutting up shop here in a few minutes, so will you do me a favour and pop into
the cleaner's next door and ask Sally for a
pound's worth of silver? Here's a pound
note. I'll have the coffee ready for you when
you get back.'

Neil rushed into the cleaner's next door
and said:

'Please could the man in the grocer's have
a pound's worth of silver, so he has enough
change to buy a programme on his way into
the match?'

Sally took the pound note and said:

'Yes, I'll get it for you, love.'

Then she looked at Neil and said:

'But that reminds me – I'll be shutting up the shop in half a jiffy, so I can go to the match with my hubby. We're leaving the baby with Grandma. Will you do me a favour and nip into the sweet shop next door and buy me half a pound of peppermint bon-bons, the soft ones, for Grandma?'

Neil felt as though he would never get back. His Dad might be growing worried – and whatever happened, Neil was determined not to miss the match. Still, he dashed into the sweet shop and asked for half a pound of peppermint bon-bons, the soft ones.

'Righto, dearie,' said the girl, lifting down the jar. 'Now, while I weigh these out for you, will you just pop outside and see if it looks like rain? I'm going to shut up shop in a minute and go to the match, but I'm not sure whether to take my brolly with me.'

Neil ran outside and looked up at the sky. It was bright blue, and there wasn't a cloud to be seen. He ran back into the shop.

'It won't rain,' he said. 'I don't think you need to take your brolly.'

'Oh, thank you, dearie,' said the girl, 'then I shan't. Here's the bon-bons and here's your change. Might see you at the match.'

Neil hurried back to the cleaner's and said:

'Here's your bon-bons and here's your change.'

'Oh, thank you, love,' said the girl in the cleaner's. 'I'll be getting back to Grandma and the baby. Here's your pound's worth of silver. Might see you at the match.'

Neil took the silver back to the grocer.

'Here's your silver,' he said.

'Ah, thanks, laddie,' said the grocer. 'And here's your jar of coffee and your change. I'll be shutting up shop now and then I'll be off to make sure I'm in time to get a programme. Might see you at the match.'

Neil took the coffee and the change and ran next door to the newsagent's.

'Here's your coffee and your change,' he said.

'Ah, thanks, sonny,' said the newsagent. 'Here's your change and your paper with all today's sport in. I'll be locking up now and getting back home with this coffee, so my wife can get my flask ready. Might see you at the match.'

Neil took the paper, and the change from the fifty pence piece, and raced back home as fast as he could. His Dad was waiting for him.

'Shan't be a minute, Dad,' said Neil breathlessly. He ran through the house, out of the back door and into the back yard. He scrambled up on to the dustbin and peered over the back wall. The barge-man was standing on the towpath looking at his barge, which was now tied to a post. He was holding Neil's football under one arm.

'I've got your paper and the change,' called Neil.

'Ah, thanks,' said the man. 'And here's your football. It's a bit wet, but it'll soon dry on a nice sunny day like this.'

He gave Neil the football and Neil reached down to give him the newspaper and the change. The man handed the change back to him.

'No,' he said. 'You keep it. You can buy

yourself a programme or some crisps at the match. I might see you there. 'Bye now.'

''Bye,' called Neil, 'and thank you.'

He climbed down and ran into the house to tell his Dad he was ready at last. They set off to walk to the football ground, and it took Neil nearly twenty minutes to tell his Dad the whole story of how he got his football back. I wonder if you can remember exactly how he did it . . .

The Autograph

One Saturday afternoon Mark was sitting back in an armchair feeling really upset. One leg was in plaster and it was resting on a cushion on a stool in front of him.

'I'm fed up,' he said to his mother.

'Never mind,' she said. 'Broken legs get better, you know. Now why don't you watch the football on television, while I go in the kitchen and make a cake for tea? Shall I switch on for you?'

'No,' frowned Mark. He was still upset. Fancy falling off his bike and breaking his leg. And it would have to happen just when his Dad and his big brother, Steve, had promised to take him to a real football match. His first real football match, in the stadium, and with Vince Oliver playing. Dad's sports paper called Vince Oliver 'the fastest thing on two legs' – and the match was today, and he was going to have to miss it, because of his broken leg.

'I'm fed up,' said Mark again.

'Never mind,' said his Dad. 'I'll bring you my programme back, and I bet they'll be showing the match on telly later this evening. I'll ask Mum to let you stay up to see it.'

'I'm still fed up,' said Mark.

Steve came in with an ice-cream.

'Here you are,' he said. 'I've just bought it for you off Sam's van. He asked how you were, and I said you were fed up because you were missing the match. So he put an extra sprinkle of nuts on top and stuck an extra chocolate flake in – said it was Sam's Special and it would cheer you up.'

Now Mark had to smile and began to lick the ice-cream.

'We'll have to go now, son,' said his Dad, coming in with his red and white scarf around his neck. 'I won't forget your programme.'

'And I tell you what,' said Steve, 'I'll try to get Vince Oliver's autograph for you. His very own name, written by himself in his very own handwriting—how about that?'

11

Mark felt really cheerful now, and waved goodbye to them and let his mother switch on the television for him, while he enjoyed his Sam's Special. He watched television most of that Saturday afternoon. Then his leg began to itch, and because there was plaster on it, he couldn't get at it to scratch it. Then he began to get stiff sitting in the same position in the same chair for hours on end.

'I hate this plaster,' he said to his mother when she came in to see how he was.

'Never mind,' she said.

Everybody seems to be saying that to me today, thought Mark. But I *do* mind. I don't want a rotten plaster on my leg. I want to be at the match with Steve and Dad. I want to see Vince Oliver play.

'Will you come in the kitchen and ice the top of the cake for me, Mark?' asked his mother. 'I'll let you use the icer to make squiggly patterns, if you like.'

Mark sniffed, then cheered up and hopped into the kitchen on his good leg. He had to hold on to chairs and doorposts to help him. Then his mother helped him up on to a high stool to do the icing.

When his Dad and Steve got in, he could see that their team had won. They both looked pleased. Dad was smiling and Steve was chanting:

'Up the Reds! Up the R-e-ds!'

'Here's the programme,' said Dad, handing it to Mark. 'We won: three–nil.'

'Did you see Vince Oliver?' asked Mark.

'Course,' said Steve. 'He got two of the goals. Guess what, though – near the end of the match he was tackled and he fell against one of the goal posts. They had to help him off.'

'Hey, I hope he's not badly hurt,' said Mark. 'So you didn't get his autograph?'

'No, sorry, I'll try next time he's playing.'

But they found out later that Vince Oliver was to be out of football for some time; he had broken his arm.

Two weeks later Mark had to go back to the hospital. The doctor wanted to see his leg and put on a new plaster. He sat with his Mum in the waiting room. A nurse came in.

'Mark Foster, your turn, please.'

Mark and his Mum went into a little room where another nurse cut down the side of his plaster with a pair of specially strong scissors. After that a doctor examined his leg and said it was mending beautifully. Then the nurse put fresh plaster round his leg. His Mum pushed him back to the waiting room in a wheel-chair and they sat and waited for the plaster to dry.

'Two more weeks, Mark, and you should be playing football again,' smiled the nurse.

His Mum went over to her to make the next appointment for him. The man in

the chair next to Mark's had his arm in plaster. He had been listening.

'Do you like football, then?' he asked.

'Oh yes,' said Mark. He told the man about how he'd been going to see his first real football match when he fell off his bike and couldn't go. 'And I specially wanted to see Vince Oliver play,' said Mark, 'so when I had to stay at home, my brother said he'd get his autograph, but he couldn't, because Vince broke his arm.'

'Yes,' said the man with the arm in plaster. 'Yes, I did.'

15

'*You* did?' said Mark. He stared. 'You? Are you Vince Oliver? But you're not like my pictures of you. You're not in your football things.'

'No, I only wear them for training and for matches,' laughed Vince. 'Usually I wear ordinary clothes. That's why you didn't recognize me. You're used to seeing pictures of me in red and white.'

Mark was so amazed, he couldn't speak. He just stared and stared. Vince Oliver, *the* Vince Oliver, was sitting on the chair next to him. He couldn't believe it.

'Tell you what,' said Vince. 'I can still write with my left hand. Would you like my autograph now – or is it too late?'

Mark could only shake his head. Vince took a pen from his pocket and bent down over Mark's leg. Mark squinted sideways to watch. Vince was writing:

'From one footballer to another. All the best, Vince Oliver.'

The plaster was taken off two weeks later. When the nurse had removed it, Mark said, 'I want to keep that, please. It's my autograph from Vince.'

The nurse looked very surprised, but she gave it back to him. Now it's hanging on Mark's bedroom wall for everyone to see. A little label is pinned next to it. It reads:

'The fastest thing on two legs autographed this for the slowest thing on one leg.'

Easy Peasy

Micky sat staring at his number book in a puzzled way, chewing the end of his pencil.

'Micky Bingham!' said Mr Gates, his class teacher. 'You're day-dreaming *again*. I wish you were as good at number work as your Sam was when he was in this class last year.'

Micky pulled his chair in and shuffled his feet. He frowned at his sums, trying to look as though he understood them. But he didn't really. They were carrying sums. Whenever he mentioned them at home, his elder brother, Sam, just said, 'Oh, carrying sums, they're easy peasy' – so he was no help.

Micky didn't understand what you had to carry or where you had to carry it to. Why did you have to *carry* it, anyway? Why couldn't you put it, or slide it, or drop it, or head it, perhaps, or kick it? In fact, he would really enjoy giving all those nasty numbers a good hefty thump with the toe of his football boot...

'Ow-aahh!' yelled Susan Porter, who was sitting opposite Micky. 'What did you go and kick me for, Micky Bingham?' she said furiously. She rubbed her knee and glared at Micky.

Mr Gates came over and put a heavy hand on Micky's shoulder.

'Now what are you up to?' he demanded. 'I must say, I never had any trouble with your Sam during the whole of last year. *And* he always got the hang of his number work straight away. In fact, he was so quick on the ball that we used to call him Speedy Sam.'

Mr Gates looked down at Micky and shook his head.

'Perhaps you'll get the hang of things one day, Micky. You're just a slow starter.'

Micky didn't answer. He just sighed helplessly. If only the weekend would come...

Saturday afternoon arrived at last. Micky was the first in the changing rooms as always, and the first of the school team out on the football field warming up. Soon his team-mates joined him, all wearing their bright yellow shirts and black shorts. They kicked a ball about until Mr Charlton, their games teacher and coach, arrived. He called them to him.

'Well, team, you know this is what we've been working for all season. We've done amazingly well to get as far as the Final. But this afternoon you've got to play better than you ever have before. If we want that Gallagher cup to stand in the school hall, we've *got* to beat Stoker School. Look, there's their coach arriving. We'd better go and meet them.'

Mr Charlton and Micky, the team captain, were the first to welcome the Stoker School team for the Final. As the opposing team came down the steps of the coach, they seemed to Micky to be bigger and stronger than any of his team, and they had a keen, determined look on their faces. They would be very hard to beat.

Soon the Stoker players were changed into their blue strip and were on the field with Micky's team, the Baxter Street School. The whistle blew. The Final had begun.

Stoker School won the ball straight away and took it away to their opponents' goal in four passes. 'Shoot!' shouted their coach. The tall player who had the ball turned to the goal, drew his foot back and kicked – wham, straight into the back of the net. Goal!

The Stoker team cheered wildly and ran back to their positions, punching the air with their fists. Micky and his team couldn't believe it – a goal against them in the first three minutes!

They managed to gain the ball and take it into the Stoker half of the field. Then a broad-shouldered Stoker boy tackled Jimmy Rees, making him stumble. Meanwhile, the ball had been turned and sent flying back to the Baxter Street end. A swift kick from a winger spun it past the back of the Baxter Street goalie and into the net.

Two goals to nil, already!

Micky could see the despairing expressions on his team-mates' faces.

'Come on, Baxter Street!' he cried encouragingly. But they were already two goals down and felt they could never recover.

Eventually the half-time whistle blew. The visiting players ran off excitedly to gather round their coach. The Baxter Street boys walked gloomily across to where Mr Charlton had towels and lemonade waiting for them. He didn't say much, but they all knew that the next half of the match was the most important of the whole season. At the end of half-time they ran back to their positions determined to play better than ever before.

The Stoker team soon had the ball and began passing it lightly from player to player; they obviously thought this match was going to be a walkover. As Micky ran past one of his opponents, he saw him wink at one of his friends, murmuring, 'Easy peasy.'

Micky suddenly grew cold and furious. How dare they think they could win as easily as that?

'Come on, team,' he yelled. 'Attack them!'

He streaked up the field, making for the Stoker player with the ball. The boy was so surprised at the sudden tackle that he let the ball go and watched Micky dribble it past the centre line and send it to one of his own team. It was passed to and fro on the wing, and then little Billy Wiley tapped it across the front of the net and over the goal line. A goal at last!

The Baxter Street boys renewed their attack. They began to defend more vigorously and to block the ball every time it came anywhere near their penalty area. After ten minutes of mid-field passing on both sides, the game seemed to be at a standstill. Then Jimmy Rees managed to tackle the broad-shouldered Stoker player who had made him stumble in the first half. This time it was Jimmy who won the ball and sent it hurtling past the stunned Stoker goalkeeper, straight into a corner of the net. The equalizer!

Two all.

The Baxter Street players began to play more confidently now. They were putting pressure on the Stoker team, who were looking anxious for the first time.

'Keep it up, Baxter Boys!' shouted Micky. He felt as though his energy would never give out; he'd be able to keep running all day. He'd give those Stoker boys "easy peasy". Five minutes to go. The ball came across the field to Micky. Out of the corner of his eye, he saw one of the blue team racing to head off the ball. Micky put on a burst of speed and reached the ball first. He sent it flying down the wing to Jimmy Rees, who kicked it across to little Billy Wiley. Six blue players closed in on him, and Billy looked wildly round for an opening. Micky streaked towards him and Billy tapped the ball over. Micky trapped it, turned swiftly and dribbled it past the helpless Stoker players.

The Stoker goalie was standing waiting, legs apart, ready to beat off anything that

came at him. Micky dribbled the ball past the goal mouth. The goalie relaxed, thinking the danger was over. But Micky gave the ball an unexpected flick with the back of his heel. Whoooosshh! The ball shot into the side of the net, then rolled to the goalie's feet. It was a goal. Three–two.

'Goal, goal, goal!' roared the Baxter Street supporters. Mr Charlton was waving both arms wildly in the air. The Baxter boys were jubilant; they were in the lead at last, thanks to Micky – and there was the final whistle!

'Three cheers for Micky!' they shouted, and closed round him, slapping him on the back and yelling excitedly. Sam had been watching on the touchline.

'That was dead ace, Micky,' he said. 'Wish I could play football like you.'

The referee called for silence and Councillor Gallagher stepped forward from among the spectators.

'Well done, Stoker School,' he said. 'You were splendid losers. And very well done, Baxter Street School – I've never seen such a remarkable recovery from a slow start. That was a great Final. And now I'd like to present the Gallagher cup to your captain.'

Micky stepped forward. The Councillor beamed at him.

'Congratulations, Micky, for a marvellous last goal. That was one of the most exciting finishes to a match that I've ever seen.'

He shook Micky's hand and presented him with the gleaming silver cup. Micky held it up for everyone to see.

'Hurray!' shouted the Baxter Street team and their supporters. 'Hurray for Baxter Street and Micky Bingham – hurray, 'ray, 'ray.'

A Treat for Donna

Every week Donna stood on the front step and scowled. 'Why can't I come with you?' she sulked.

'Because you're not old enough,' her big sister, Val, always said.

'How about if we take you swimming tomorrow?' said Brian. He always tried to cheer Donna up. She liked him. He was Val's boy-friend.

'Oh, come on, Bri,' said Val, 'or we'll be late for the kick-off.'

Next week it was just the same. Donna caught them trying to slip off to the football without telling her.

'Can I come?' she demanded.

'No, you can't,' said Val. 'Go and call for one of your friends.'

'Why can't I come with you?' pouted Donna.

'Because you're not old enough,' said Val. 'Go on, buzz off.'

'When will I be old enough, then?' asked Donna.

'When your next birthday comes,' said Brian. 'We'll take you with us then, won't we, Val?'

'Oh, all right then,' said Val. 'When your next birthday comes, we'll take you – OK?'

'Ooh, thanks, that's brill!' Donna ran to tell her mother what Val and Brian had promised.

When it was nearly her birthday, she looked for the day on the calendar. She was quite upset when she saw that it wasn't to be a Saturday, when Brian and Val usually went to watch football.

'That doesn't matter,' said Brian. 'Look, it's going to be a Wednesday. That's when the Rovers often play an evening game. You'll enjoy that. I'm sure your Mum'll let you stay up late just for once, as it's your birthday.'

The birthday Wednesday came at last. They had Donna's favourite tea: poached eggs on toast, followed by strawberry trifle, and a slice of birthday cake as well. Val looked at the clock.

'Come on, you two,' she said. 'We'd better get going. Put plenty on, Donna, it gets cold at these evening matches.'

Donna pulled on her quilted coat and her mitts.

'I've filled the flask with tea,' said Val, coming out of the kitchen. Brian put it into the pocket of his duffle coat. Donna's Mum gave her a bag of mints.

'They'll help to keep you warm,' she said. 'Now look after her, you two. She's not used to being out so late and in those crowds.'

They went out into the darkness. The air was cold and smelt frosty. Donna walked between Val and Brian, trying to keep up with them. As they came nearer to the Rovers' football ground, more and more people were hurrying along, coming from all the side streets round about to join the crowd, all going in the same direction. Donna took hold of Brian's duffle coat – she didn't want to get lost. All round was the sound of thousands of feet hurrying along; in the distance

they could hear a faint sort of roar and the sound of muffled music.

'Here we are,' said Brian. 'We have to go through this turnstile here. One at a time, Donna. Get behind me.'

He stood and paid for the tickets, then pushed through the turnstile, clack-clack-clack-clack. Then Donna pushed through, followed by Val. They went up some stone steps and there, suddenly, was the football ground.

High up above the ground huge dazzling lights shone down. Round the sides of the long green pitch were rows and rows of stone steps which went up and up like stairs. On these steps were standing hundreds of people; Donna had never seen so many in her life. Everyone was talking and laughing, and loud music was playing over loud-speakers.

'Along here,' said Brian. 'We've got seats.'

They walked along one of the stone steps to where there were rows of wooden seats, each row higher than the one below, so that everyone had a good view of the pitch. They sat down.

'Just in time,' said Val. 'Here come the Rovers.'

The crowd broke into an excited roar as the home team, dressed in white, ran on to the green turf. They were followed by the referee in black, two linesmen with their flags, and the visiting team, City, all in orange.

Peeeeeeep! The referee blew his whistle and the game started. Donna kept her eyes on the Rovers; she wanted them to win. Every time one of the City team managed to get the ball, she groaned and held her breath.

Both teams raced up and down the field, never looking tired or breathless. Donna knew she couldn't have kept running like that – she'd soon have had stitch and had to stop.

'Oh, help!' she yelled. City had the ball and were racing towards the Rovers' goal. She jumped to her feet. 'Oh, no!' she cried.

'Goal!' groaned the Rovers' supporters. 'Now they're one up.'

Val pulled her back down on to her seat.

'Don't worry,' she said. 'Rovers will aim to score an equalizer by half-time.'

Val was right. Ten minutes later the white team took the ball up the side of the field, passed it across to the centre and – wham!

'Beautiful!' yelled Brian, leaping to his feet.

'Hurray-ay-ay!' shouted Val, jumping up too.

'Great!' shouted Donna, but she couldn't hear herself shouting, as the Rovers' supporters all round roared and cheered. The half-time whistle went. One–all. An excited hum of talk broke out as the players walked off the field. Announcements were given over the loudspeakers. Brian poured drinks of steaming tea from the flask. Val brought a bag of crisps from her pocket and shared them with Donna. Brian stood up.

'Shan't be long,' he said, 'I just want a word with a friend.'

Donna stared round at the crowd. There was so much to look at — supporters in their scarves and rosettes, men reading football programmes or the sports paper, boys selling pies and drinks, people chatting or walking up and down to keep warm. Donna had never seen so many people together in her life. Brian came back. Suddenly there came an announcement over the loudspeaker.

'Ladies and gentlemen. I believe we have a very special guest here this evening — someone who has never been to a football match before in her life. Donna Pritchard — yes, it's little Donna Pritchard's first time here at the Rovers' ground, and she asked to come here specially tonight as a birthday treat. So, ladies and gentlemen — here's our greeting to Donna Pritchard!'

The announcement stopped and music came over the air instead.

'It's "Happy Birthday to you",' gasped Donna. People all round were humming and singing along with the tune. Val and Brian were laughing and singing too. Donna was amazed; she could feel herself going very red.

'How did they know?' she asked. 'How did they know?'

Then the players were running back on to the pitch. Play began. The ball was sent up and down the field, but there were no more goals.

'Come on, the whites!' yelled Donna.

A few minutes later one of the orange team gave the ball a terrific thump. It flew through the air, over the sideline and towards their seats. It fell just where Donna was sitting. It was slippery and dirty with mud, but she managed to hold on to it and fling it back to one of the Rovers who had the throw-in.

Once again the players raced to and fro. Only ten minutes to go. They were getting tired and weren't running quite so fast. Donna was growing tired too; she rested her head against Val's arm, and felt her eyes closing.

'Hey, look at that,' said Brian. Donna shot forward in her seat. One of the Rovers was racing up the centre of the field. The City players were closing in on him, but he dodged them and booted the ball to a team-mate, who tapped it smartly over the line and into the back of the net.

'It's a goal!' yelled everyone. Brian waved his arms in the air and cheered.

'Hurray! Goal! Goal!' shouted Val and Donna, standing up and cheering again and again. The crowd was really excited now and very noisy. Gradually they calmed down again. People began to whistle, to remind the referee that time was nearly up. The players walked back to their places on the field and – Peeeeep-peeeeep! The final whistle blew.

They hurried back home through the cold night air. Donna held on to Val's arm on one side and Brian's on the other.

'Two—one to the Rovers – that's terrific,' said Val. 'Usually, City's a hard team to beat.'

'You must have brought Rovers luck, Donna,' said Brian.

'It was fantastic,' said Donna. 'Really great, thanks for taking me. It was the best treat I could possibly have had. But I still don't know how they knew it was my birthday. Wasn't it peculiar?'

'Yes,' said Val. 'It was.'

'Yes, very peculiar,' said Brian. 'How did they find out?'

You Win Some,
You Lose Some

Joey went into the greengrocer's.

'Six pounds of onions,' he said.

'You sure, sonny?' asked the greengrocer. 'Six pounds seems an awful lot of onions. Perhaps it was just six onions your mother wanted?'

'They're not for my mother, they're for my big brother,' said Joey. 'And he wanted six pounds. That's what he said: six pounds of onions.'

'All right, all right,' said the greengrocer, and weighed out the fat round onions in their papery brown skins. Joey paid him and carried the bag home.

'Got them?' asked Eddie. 'Right, bring them over here and spread them on this newspaper. We'll chop them before we go. You take this knife, Joey, and cut them in half and pull the outside skins off. I'll have the sharpest knife and slice them really fine.'

They set to work. Joey was at one end of the kitchen table, cutting the onions in half; Eddie stood opposite him with a large chopping board in front of him, chopping the halves into tiny pieces. He worked so fast, the blade of his knife flashed as he chopped.

'How do you do it so quickly?' asked Joey, full of admiration.

'Been doing it every Saturday and Wednesday for years, haven't I?' said Eddie. 'Practice makes perfect. This is the first time I've let you help, so no wonder you're slow.'

He watched as Joey cut down through an onion, his face red with the effort of pressing the blade down.

'Now what's the matter?' he asked, as he noticed a tear trickling down Joey's face.

'Nothing,' said Joey. 'Nothing at all.'

'Is it too hard for you? Is the knife blunt?' asked Eddie. 'Don't you want to come and help me today?'

'Yes, yes, of course I do,' said Joey. More tears welled up and trickled down his cheeks. 'You know I want to help you and

38

watch the match and see Wally Watson play for United.'

His face was wet with tears now. He sniffed and dashed away the tears with his sleeve.

'What is it, then, Joey?' asked Eddie. 'You must tell me what's upsetting you.'

'I don't know,' blinked Joey. 'My eyes just started to cry on their own.'

Eddie looked at him. Then he suddenly realized what the matter was.

'Oh, of course – it's the onions,' he said. 'Slicing onions makes some people's eyes water. Not mine, though. I expect my eyes have got used to it over the years. But I bet that's what it is, Joey – it's the onions. Why don't you leave them to me to finish off now? You can go and load the rolls and the sausages into the van.'

Joey wiped his eyes again and went across to where trays of long bread rolls were stacked up on top of one another, and large polythene bags full of fresh sausages lay ready. He picked up a bag of sausages and walked outside with it to where Eddie's van stood, its back door wide open. He started to load up. In ten minutes Eddie had finished cutting the onions and had filled a polythene bag with them. He put them in the back of the van and checked that everything else had been loaded.

'Come on, then, Joey,' he said. 'Time's getting on, let's get moving.'

They drove off through the town traffic, under the railway bridge, past the station, along some cobbled streets, round a corner – and there was the football ground.

'We drive in at a special entrance,' said Eddie. 'We're not spectators, we're business.'

'On the hot dog stall,' said Joey.

'Right,' said Eddie. He backed the van up to the stall, unlocked the door and pushed up the shutters. They unloaded everything.

'Here, put this white overall on,' said Eddie, 'while I get the sausages and onions going.'

Soon a delicious smell rose from the cooker: hot sausages and onions.

'You have to ask the customers if they want tomato sauce or mustard as well,' said Eddie. 'And put the money in this tin.'

People started to walk past their stall. Some of them stopped as they smelt the savoury smell. Some of them read the painted notice above the stall: "Eddie's Hot Dogs".

Click-clack-click-clack. Now lots of people were pushing through the turnstiles. There was quite a crowd round the stall, enjoying a hot dog or two before the match. Joey was working hard, putting the hot sausages between two halves of bread rolls, piling on hot onions, slapping on dollops of mustard or tomato sauce and handing them over to the customers on paper plates. The money tin was nearly full. At last the crowds drifted away. A whistle blew. The match had begun.

'OK – take off your overall and nip up those steps,' said Eddie. 'You'll have a good view up there. Be back here straight after the whistle for half-time.'

The first half was really exciting. By half-time United were two goals up, both goals scored by Wally Watson, United's most famous player. Joey ran down the steps two at a time back to the hot dog stall.

'That was great!' he said to his brother. He put on his overall again and set to work. The first half had made people hungry, they were ready to eat a snack and talk about Wally Watson's terrific play. When the whistle for the second half went, Joey's arms were aching with all the reaching out and stretching across the counter.

'Right, off you go again,' said Eddie.

Joey raced back up the steps. This time the Rovers scored a goal in the first minute. That was bad news for United. Then, one of the Rovers team took a free-kick. The ball

spun high over the heads of United's defence, past the outstretched fingers of the goalkeeper – and into the net. United two–Rovers two.

There was a dismayed hubbub from the crowd of United supporters. Joey began to feel really miserable. The afternoon was getting colder now and dusk was coming. Only a quarter of an hour to go. United fought bravely, but Rovers were just too good for them. They got two more goals. Now the score was two–four to the Rovers.

The ball was kicked high up the field towards the United goal. Wally Watson raced forward to head it; so did one of the Rovers. Wally managed to get his head to it first, but as he jumped, he fell against the other player and they landed in a heap. The other player got up, but Wally lay on the grass, groaning. The referee bent over him, then signalled to the coach to come on. He took one look at Wally and called for a stretcher – poor Wally had a suspected broken leg. The referee looked at his watch and blew the final whistle. Four goals to the Rovers, two to United.

Poor Joey. He went slowly down the steps, one by one. He felt so miserable; he didn't think he'd ever felt so miserable before. Four to the Rovers – two to United. *And* if Wally Watson had a broken leg that would put him out of the game for months. Poor Joey. He'd been looking forward so much to coming to the match and helping Eddie and seeing United win. He sniffed and swallowed hard.

'Never mind,' said Eddie, taking a look at his little brother. 'That's football. You win some, you lose some. United have just had an off-day. They'll play again next week and they'll probably win. Don't cry, Joey.'

Joey sniffed and swallowed again.

'I'm not crying,' he said in an odd sort of voice. 'I'm not crying at all. I think it was just cutting those silly old onions.'

He gulped.

'Slicing onions always makes some people's eyes water. You said so.'

'So I did,' said Eddie. 'Silly old onions!'

Yewchurch Plays Football

Mrs Millington turned round from the piano and stood up. She looked at all the children in her little school and smiled.

'You sang very nicely this morning, children,' she said. 'And now, before you go to your classrooms, I've an important letter to tell you about.'

She took a sheet of paper from the top of the piano.

'It's from a headmaster friend of mine in the town. He thought it would be a nice idea if a football team from his school came to play against our village school football team here in Yewchurch. They could come next Friday after school. He says they're a crack team and have won lots of cups.'

At this piece of news everyone started talking.

'But we haven't got a football team,' said Miss Bevan.

'No,' said Mrs Millington. 'We'll have to find one before next Friday! Surely we can find nine? ten? – how many players are there in a football team, Miss Bevan?'

'Eleven, usually,' said Miss Bevan.

'But we've only got eleven boys in the juniors all together,' said Tommy Marsh-field, joining in.

'Ssshh, quiet Tommy,' said Miss Bevan, 'We'll talk about it later.'

They did talk about the football match later, in fact they talked of little else. They wondered how they could possibly play against a smart team from the town – Yewchurch village school was very small indeed. But the eleven boys in the juniors were keen to take part. They gathered round the headmistress in the playground later.

'Go on, Mrs Millington, write and tell him we'll have a go,' they said.

'But you've never played in a proper match before,' she said anxiously.

'Yeh, but we can practise between now

and next Friday. We've seen matches on the telly – we'll soon get the hang of it.'

Milly Patience was quite envious of her twin brother, Tony.

'You lucky duck,' she said. 'You boys get all the best chances. I'm just as good at games as you are, and I nearly always beat you at running. I wish they were bringing a girls' team to play rounders instead.'

Friday arrived. Ten of the Yewchurch team woke early, looking forward to playing in their first real football match. The eleventh player, Tony Patience, hadn't slept much at all – he'd been awake most of the night with horrible toothache. His mother phoned the dentist first thing in the morning. The earliest appointment she could make was for two o'clock. She turned to Milly.

'When you get to school, go straight to Mrs Millington and tell her about Tony's bad tooth. Say he'll come into school ready to play when he's been to the dentist's.'

Mrs Millington understood and said she hoped Tony would feel better soon. But at three o'clock there was still no sign of him.

Milly was very anxious about her brother; so were the rest of the team.

'He's our fastest sprinter,' they said, 'and he's good at dribbling with the ball. Besides, we can't play football with only ten in the team.'

Suddenly a look-out shouted:

'They're coming up the lane, here they come!'

Everyone rushed outside to watch. A bright orange van was coming up the lane. Faces were pressed against all the van windows, and from the back and sides streamed bright orange scarves. As it drew up outside, they could read the large black words on the side. CITY SUPERS. The visitors climbed out, dressed in orange shirts and shorts, chanting, 'Up-the-Su-pers! Up-the-Su-pers!'

The Yewchurch children were dumbfounded. They had never heard football chanting in the village before, and they had never thought of having special team colours – they just wore any old T-shirt and shorts. Mrs Millington stepped forward and welcomed the visitors. Then she led the way round the back of the school to the games field. The two teams followed, so did all the other children in the school who had stayed behind to watch. There was still no sign of Tony.

But then Milly caught sight of her mother hurrying up the lane and she ran out to meet her. They went into the school together and had a little chat with Miss Bevan, who was preparing refreshments ready for after the match.

Two minutes later Tony ran on to the games field.

'At last!' said everyone. 'Now we can get started.'

'Ah – Tony,' said Mrs Millington. 'How's the tooth?'

'Doesn't hurt a bit,' said Tony.

The players took up their positions. The referee looked round to see if everyone was ready. Miss Bevan came out to watch and started to say something, but Mrs Millington poked her in the ribs with her elbow.

'Shush, don't say a word,' she said. 'The game's starting.'

The City Supers seemed like enormous orange giants who raced at the Yewchurch players and surrounded them, tackling closely and quite frightening some of the smaller ones. But now and then one of the visitors would stumble and trip over, falling into the long grass.

'They're not used to jumping over the tussocks of thistles like we are,' said Tony.

One of the Supers won the ball and raced up the pitch with it. It looked as though he'd be bound to score the first goal. But at that moment Frankie Marshfield's dog raced on to the pitch, barking wildly. The City Super swerved and the ball sailed into the hedge.

'Go home, Rats!' shouted Frankie Marshfield, but his dog just stood on the sideline, wagging its tail happily.

Again a Super got control of the ball and dodged up the field with it. He stood back to take aim and the dog burst into a frenzy of barking.

'Rats!' shouted all the Yewchurch players. The Super's kick wobbled nervously and the ball spun sideways into the stream behind the goal. When the ball was kicked back up the field, it showered the players with drops of water.

Then Frankie tackled a Super, won the ball and sent it across to his friend, Doug. As usual, the orange giants raced towards the player with the ball. So with a grin, Doug kicked it into a patch of rough grass near the sideline. Two Supers raced after it.

'That's marshy!'

'Mind the bog!' came Yewchurch warnings. But too late. The Supers had run straight into it.

'Yee-ughhh!' they exclaimed in disgust, as the mud closed over their ankles and smart orange socks. They waded out, shaking dol-

lops of mud from their feet. But now a mood of determination took hold of the Supers. They roared up the field with the ball — thump, kick, wham — and the ball sailed into the back of the net. Nil to Yewchurch, one to the City Supers.

It was half-time. The orange giants gathered round their teacher to talk about tactics; the Yewchurch team went over to Rats and made a great fuss of him. Miss Bevan brought both teams some lemonade.

The whistle went for the second half. The Supers wanted a second goal; Yewchurch wanted their first. They worked hard, hurtling over tussocks of grass to beat the Supers to the ball, tackling them bravely and kicking the ball as often as possible towards their goal. At last Frankie saw an opening between two orange figures and shot hard.

'Goal, goal, goal!' cried all the Yewchurch supporters and players. One-all.

Both teams were playing well now. But time was passing — only seven minutes to go. Then the ball shot over the hedge into the field beyond. Little Tina Simons opened the gate and raced to get the ball. Yewchurch

throw-in. Doug passed it to Tony. The orange Supers began to close in, then came a sudden cry –

'Cows!'

They were advancing through the open gateway, swishing their tails and making straight for the football pitch. The Supers stopped dead in their tracks, terrified. Tony saw his chance and kicked hard – thump!

'Goal!' shouted the Yewchurch supporters, dancing up and down at the side. Two–one to Yewchurch! And then the final whistle went. Everyone clapped and cheered and shook the visitors by the hand and said what a good game it had been. Miss Bevan went over to little Tina Simons.

'I saw you leave that gate open,' she said.

'Me, Miss Bevan?' said Tina. 'I went to get the ball.'

'Yes, I know you did, and you left the gate open *and* you gave one of your father's cows a smack to get her to follow you. I saw you,' said Miss Bevan, and she turned and winked at Tina. Then she went over to Tony, who was still breathless but happy after scoring the final goal.

'Well done, Milly,' she said.

'No one guessed, did they?' said Milly.

'No, you looked just like Tony out there in Tony's T-shirt,' smiled Miss Bevan. 'It's a good thing you twins look so alike!'

'Poor old Tony,' said Milly. 'I'd better go home and tell him the good news. Mum said he was a bit groggy after having gas at the dentist's. Oh, look, the City Supers are getting back into their van. I'll just go and wave goodbye.'

She ran across to the van. The Supers' teacher recognized her and said:

'That was a good last goal. Well done, lad!'

'Oh, thank you,' said Milly, and grinned.